Lionel Arthur Tollemache

Recollections of Pattison

Lionel Arthur Tollemache

Recollections of Pattison

ISBN/EAN: 9783337219031

Printed in Europe, USA, Canada, Australia, Japan

Cover: Foto ©Andreas Hilbeck / pixelio.de

More available books at **www.hansebooks.com**

RECOLLECTIONS

OF

PATTISON.

BY THE

Hon. LIONEL A. TOLLEMACHE.

Reprinted with additions from the " Journal of Education " for June, 1885.

LONDON:

PRINTED, FOR PRIVATE CIRCULATION, BY

C. F. HODGSON & SON, GOUGH SQUARE,

FLEET STREET.

1885.

RECOLLECTIONS OF PATTISON.

"Spectateur dans l'univers, le penseur sait que le monde ne lui appartient que comme sujet d'étude, et que le rôle de réformateur suppose presque toujours en ceux qui se le donnent des défauts et des qualités qu'il n'a pas."—RENAN.

IT was at Biarritz, in March, 1882, that I made Pattison's acquaintance.* I saw much of him then, and again, six months later, when he came to join me in Switzerland. In June, 1883, we met for the last time. He took most kindly to me from the first, and in our conversations he spoke with an absence of reserve which I understand to have been unusual with him. It will, however, be seen that my personal intercourse with him was confined to a short period. I have been fortunate in obtaining the help of several of his oldest friends, who have enabled me to make my portrait of him less imperfect. In the following sketch I propose to discuss fully one aspect of his character, which seems to me to be misunderstood; in other matters, I shall as far as

* Mr. Althaus, in his very interesting and appreciative Essay on Pattison, refers to this visit, and to the philosophical dialogues of which Biarritz was the scene.

B

possible restrict myself to a record of some of his opinions and characteristic sayings, so as to let him be his own interpreter.

One more personal detail by way of preface. The Rector took an unmerited interest in my Essays (contributed chiefly to the *Fortnightly Review*); and he insisted that I should publish them in a collected form, or else print them for private circulation, or at any rate that I should inform him of the names and dates of the articles, so that he might procure copies. For private reasons I chose the second alternative: my two volumes, *Safe Studies* and *Stones of Stumbling*, are at present unpublished; but copies of them (besides being thrown broadcast among friends) have been presented to the chief public libraries,* and are thus made accessible to readers. I am obliged to mention these facts, since a few of the Rector's sayings, which will be quoted, relate to passages in those volumes.

Wishing to learn the present state of Oxford, I observed to Pattison that in my time (1856-60) most of the able undergraduates were strong

* As two friendly reviewers of my volumes have urged me to publish them, I should like to mention that they have been presented to the British Museum, the Bodleian, the Cambridge University, the Oxford and Cambridge Unions, the three University Clubs in London, the Athenæum, the Savile and Albemarle Clubs, the Royal Institution, and the London Library. Copies will be sent to any public library, on application to the publisher of the *Journal of Education*.

Liberals, both in politics and in theology, and I asked whether the same could be said of the present generation of undergraduates. In reply, he told me, doubtless with some exaggeration, that the opinions of the undergraduates are in chronic opposition to those of their tutors. It takes about twenty years for a budding student to grow into a full-blown don. Whence it follows that there are cycles of about forty years, during half of which the University rises in Liberalism, while during the other half it falls; or rather, the dons and the undergraduates are at the opposite ends of an intellectual seesaw, so that while the former are rising the latter are falling, and *vice versâ*. "When you were at Oxford," he said to me, "all the good men were Liberals; *they couldn't help it*. But now it is all changed. Many of the able undergraduates are Conservative; and those of an original turn take up Æstheticism"!

One who was his pupil in 1850 writes:—

" In my own case, the greatest piece of intellectual insight he showed was in persuading me to give up Natural Science as my main pursuit. 'You care for the literature of science, and for the results of science; you don't really care for science itself. You read Bacon and Herschel's *Introduction*, and the *Vestiges*, and Humboldt's *Cosmos;* but you don't come into chapel with the mud of Shotover and the railway cuttings sticking to your knees.' "

The same pupil told Pattison, rather apologetically, that, having been brought up in Scotland, he had never learnt the Greek Grammar, but had only used it as a book of reference. "I am delighted to hear it," was the unexpected reply; "far too much time is wasted on the Greek grammar." This view of Pattison's was all the more remarkable, because it was expressed thirty-five years ago.

I learn from the same source that Pattison (then sub-Rector) said to some of his most hardworking pupils, "I will let you off my lectures on Thursdays, on condition that you promise to make the day a complete holiday." He evidently thought that more intellectual good, or less physical harm, would follow from hard work for (say) six hours a day for five days in the week, than from hard work for five hours a day for six days.

A more recent pupil, intending to write for a Prize Essay, was urged by the Rector to begin at once: " No amount of hurried reading at the end will take the place of the process of slow gestation." Pattison might have said (employing Mr. Galton's metaphor) that a writer's thoughts ought to be long kept within call in " the antechamber of consciousness," before they are summoned to the presence chamber. The principle involved in the above advice was a favourite one with him. He always insisted that any one engaged in literary work ought, for the time being, to give up all practical avocations. He, of course, did not forget that Bacon, Macaulay, and countless others attained great literary success amid the distractions of public life; but he would probably have contended that those giants, had they been able to devote themselves exclusively to literature, might have attained a yet greater success, and that ordinary mortals, if they do not so devote themselves, will attain no success at all.

Certainly his standard of the requirements of a literary life was rigid to the verge of pedantry. A very able (and far too penitent) friend of his writes:

"He suggested that I should edit Selden's *Table Talk*. The preparation was to be, first to get the contents practically by heart, then to read the whole printed literature of Selden's day, and of the generation before him. In twenty years he promised me that I should be prepared for the work. He put the thing before me in so unattractive a way that I never did it or anything else worth doing. I consider the ruin of my misspent life very largely due to that conversation."

That this severe judgment on the Rector may not be taken too literally, I will quote from the same letter, "He was one of the best friends I ever had. He was not in the least donnish when one came to know him."

One learns without surprise that, in the words of a near relation, "he had a quite human fondness for his books; nothing annoyed him so much as to hear one of them fall; and dusting them, which he reduced to a science, seemed to give him real pleasure. In his last illness the sight of any of his favourites depressed him greatly. 'Ah!' he would say, 'I am to leave my books,' and sometimes, 'They have been more to me than my friends.' He would ask for them one after the other, till he was literally covered almost to his shoulders as he lay, and the floor around him was strewn with them. He used to say that the sight of books was necessary to him at his work; and, once reading how Schiller always kept 'rotten apples' in his study because their scent was beneficial to him, he pointed to some shelves above his head, where he kept his oldest and most prized editions, and said: 'There are my rotten apples.'"

Such severe comments are often passed on clergymen who accept the dogmas of their church in a spiritual, not a literal, sense, that I feel some scruple in recording Pattison's comments on the orthodox theology. But one circumstance re-assures me. Some of us can remember only too well the consternation with which, thirteen years ago, members of London Society learnt that one of their own body, the Duke of Somerset, was in the enemy's camp, and with what refreshing ease they let themselves be convinced that Archbishop

Thomson had put the Sadducees to silence. No one at all familiar with the Rector's later writings can doubt that his judgment on this controversy might have been conveyed in Henry VI.'s words:—

"I more incline to Somerset than York."

As Pattison himself has spoken so plainly,* I need not mind speaking plainly also. Nevertheless, "Haud ignota loquor" is not my only apology for publishing what he said to me; I have obtained an assurance from those authorized to speak on his behalf that they in no wise object to the publication.

I asked him how it was that, being so very outspoken in his writings, he yet seemed never to burn his fingers, as other Broad Church clergymen did. He answered that, as a matter of fact, he had burnt his fingers, but that he would have burnt them much worse if the outspoken passages had occurred in theological writings: editors entrusted such books as the *Life of Milton* to the

---

* I have elsewhere (*Stones of Stumbling*, p. 46) quoted Grote's opinion that the success of Christianity was one of the greatest calamities that ever befell the human race. Did he mean much more by this than Pattison (Memoirs, p. 96) meant by saying that "the triumph of the Church organization over the wisdom and philosophy of the Hellenic world . . . . is, to the Humanist, the saddest moment in history— the ruin of the painfully constructed fabric of civilization to the profit of the Church"?

tender mercies of lay critics—such books as Mr. Jowett's Commentary on St. Paul to the untender mercies of clerical ones. He told me that at one period he had been on the point of turning Catholic, and that he had been deterred chiefly by observing that on political and scientific questions—the only questions which admit of being directly tested—the Catholic Church had been time after time in the wrong. He admitted that he had become much more Liberal even than he was when he sent his contribution to *Essays and Reviews.*

He was asked whether he did not think that the attempts made by Archdeacon Farrar and others to show that the eternity of punishment cannot be demonstrated from the Gospels, are utterly futile. He expressed his assent by saying, " If they can explain away the word αἰώνιος, there are perfectly clear expressions to the same effect in other texts." He was therefore of opinion that the belief in the non-eternity of punishment involves the postulate that the Master's words, as reported in the Gospels, contain errors. I had adopted the same view in an article in the *Fortnightly Review* (December, 1877). I begged him to read the article carefully through, and to tell me whether it contained anything to which rational objection could be taken. After reading it over, he found only one trifling matter to which he at all demurred.*

He used the term "economy" (that is, husbanding, *ménagement*) "of truth" to denote the practice of answering fools according to their folly, and of speaking parables to them that are without. I was so struck with the phrase that, in reprinting my article, mentioned in the last paragraph, I rechristened it "Divine Economy of Truth"; but I first wrote to ask the Rector what authority there was for the phrase which he so often employed. He answered:—

"I almost think a tract of Keble in *Tracts for the Times* was the first in our day to bring up the word 'Economy' in the sense you mean. But this was a revival, not an original invention. The Greek fathers not seldom speak of the οἰκονομίας σωτηρίου—as we say, the Christian 'dispensation.' The idea is, that revelation itself is only a veil, half revealing, half concealing, and so a test or touchstone of earnest minds, only such being willing to wait and learn. And, as God

---

* He thought that perhaps I made too much of Jer. vii. 22 (*Stones of Stumbling*, p. 102). I was glad to be informed by so comparatively orthodox a divine as Dr. Baldwin Brown that he had read my article with sympathy, and that he thought that the next step taken by the Broad Church party will perhaps be to impugn the infallibility of the words reported in the Gospels. Tillotson suggests, in Sermon xxxv., that God may have represented future punishment as more horrible than it really is to be, the exaggeration being the only possible way of deterring men from sin. Compare Selden's *Table Talk, s.v. Damnation.*

dispenses crumbs of truth to the chosen, so in the visible Church the clergy are dispensers to their flock of so much truth as they think good for them.   Keble's tract is entitled, ' On reserve in communicating religious knowledge.'   ' God punishes with mental blindness those who approach religious questions with a speculative mind ' is his dictum—the text about casting pearls before swine is dwelt upon."

A Catholic nobleman, who lived near Holywell, once gave me an extraordinary account of a man, to all appearance blind for many years, who recovered his sight after resorting to that sacred spring.   On my mentioning this incident, Pattison said, "It is seldom possible to sift the evidence in such cases.   There is only one real test.   Give the Holywell water to the inmates of a blind-asylum, and see whether it cures them." A Catholic would, of course, object that the application of such a test would imply want of faith, and that God would punish this want of faith by refusing to work the miracle.*   Pattison would have declared, and I certainly should not deny, that this objection is irrational.   I merely insist that, in pronouncing it to be irrational, we are claiming the right of transferring, not this question only, but every similar one, from the Theo-

---

* Orthodox Protestants made a similar objection to Sir Henry Thompson's proposed method of testing the objective efficacy of prayer.   I would commend to their notice two *experimenta fidei* sanctioned in the Bible : Judges vi. 36—40 ; 1 Kings xviii. 23—39.

logical to the Scientific Court of Appeal; we are making the assumption that a knowledge of natural laws is our mainstay, just as reliance on supernatural aid was the mainstay of our fathers —in a word, that " our valours are our best'gods," and that Prudence is Providence writ small.

The Rector's attention was called to the startling amount of evidence which Herodotus brings forward on behalf of portents which we now reject as a matter of course; and he was asked whether, after pondering on that evidence, he did not doubt the conclusiveness of the testimony, even of the " 500 brethren at once," which is adduced by a more famous writer in support of a far greater miracle. " What weight," asked he, " can you attach to such testimony? It rests on the *ipse dixit* of a single reporter, who places his own vision on the same level with the rest of the evidence." In reference to the prophetic, I mean *predictive*, power which is claimed for the Founders of Christianity, he made the remark: Of all the momentous events that have occurred since the destruction of Jerusalem, not one was foretold in the New Testament. He defined orthodoxy as " Stoicism *plus* a legend."

It will be convenient to speak of his political forebodings further on. At present I will merely mention that he considered political pessimism to be on the increase, and that he attributed the increase to two causes. The first cause is, the disappointment which was felt by Liberals after 1848. He exclaimed with exaggerative vehemence: "Before 1848 men expected to get everything by revolutions; they soon learnt that they were not a bit better off than before." The second cause is an indirect and negative one. Men are apt to infer from the Divine Goodness that good *must* be the final goal of ill, and that an increasing purpose *must* run through all the ages. And, as a matter of fact, men commonly hold that the nineteenth century fares (so to say) better than the eighteenth, and the eighteenth than the seventeenth; therefore, the twentieth will fare better than the nineteenth, and for evermore each $n+1^{\text{th}}$ will fare better than each nth. But, alas, this vision of an earthly Paradise men of science are ruthlessly consigning to dreamland. Either freezing or frying, they tell us, is to be the lot of our remote descendants; and this unpleasing catastrophe is likely to be ushered in by long ages of decline: during those ages each $n+1^{\text{th}}$ century will fare *worse* than each nth. Of course, this does not prove that the twentieth will fare worse than the nineteenth. But it breaks the spell of the *à priori* reasoning on which, according to Pattison, the belief in progress mainly rests; and thus it infuses into philosophers a restless unfaith—a sentiment akin to that of δῖνος βασιλεύει τὸν Δί' ἐξεληλακώς, or at least to that of

> Usque adeo res humanas vis abdita quædam
> Obterit.

A few of the Rector's literary criticisms may find a place here. Some interest may be felt in the miscellaneous intellectual diet which he pre-scribed to me in a letter (14th October, 1883) :—

"You will read Spielhagen's *Quisisana*, and Trollope's *Autobiography*. I myself find much fireside sympathy in Twining's *Reminiscences*—but it is mild tobacco, and has a special flavour of eighteenth century about it, which may not be to everyone's taste. Have you ever read A. Gellius' *Noctes Atticæ?* You will find some curious matters there, though perhaps Jevons' *Social Essays* may be more to your liking. Above all, read the speeches of the clericals at the Reading Congress—quite time for some one to rap them on the head."

He also urged me, and many other friends, to read Amiel's *Journal Intime*. May not his relish for Amiel's moral self-dissection have been due to his sympathy with one who suffered from great mental depression—depression aggravated by con-sidering how much had been expected from him, and how little he had performed ?*

To a friend who complained of not caring for the character of Æneas, Pattison observed that the interest of the Æneid is derived neither from

* See the *Note* at the end of this essay.

its characters nor from its plot, but merely from its being a Handbook of Roman Antiquities. This conversation probably occurred some years before he spoke to me on the same subject in very different terms. I understood him to say that the charm of Virgil lies in his power of exciting " successive waves of emotion " in the reader's mind. He read with very great interest Mr. Myers's Essay on the poet, which he described as something quite out of the common. He went the length of saying that, in the beauty of occasional passages, Virgil is unsurpassed by any poet, ancient or modern; and he gave as an instance the encomium on Italy (*Georg.* II. 136—176), which reaches its climax in the line,

> " Salve, magna parens frugum, Saturnia tellus,
> Magna virum."

He told me that he thought he should never like Dante, and he knew he should never like Carlyle. His aversion to Carlyle is referred to in a letter which I received from a member of his family :—

" I don't think that he cared at all about Carlyle; he used to call him a juggler with words, and to speak contemptuously of anything infected with his style. He belonged to the Browning Society, and even took the chair at one of its meetings, but he would not allow that Mr. Browning is a poet; he never read his works for pleasure, but merely to see what it was that people talked about. Wordsworth seemed to give him more pleasure than any English poet, and he loved to read Schiller's *Gedichte*. He was glad of an excuse for turning up Pope, and, if we met with a quotation from him in our reading, he would insist on finding the context, and reading it aloud with a peculiar swing and tone of voice which he always used for Pope. His delight over his favourite epigrams was most amusing. The couplet—

> ' On her white breast a sparkling cross she wore,
> Which Jews might kiss, and infidels adore.'

he was never tired of declaring to be inimitable."

He told me that, in order to enjoy Wordsworth thoroughly, I ought to be familiar with the Lake district. Indeed, he seems to have thought it extremely important to take poets (in this literal sense) on their own ground. Miss Swanwick has kindly authorized me to mention that she was somewhat amused by the persistence with which he urged her to go all the way to Sicily in order to be able to appreciate Theocritus, " an acquaintance with Sicilian scenery, and with the Sicilian people, being, in his opinion, essential for the full enjoyment of the *Idylls*." She also informs me that, on their first meeting, he opened fire by asking, " Which do you think the finest poem in the world ? " She replied that the question needed deliberation, and asked which *he* thought the finest poem. He at once answered, " The *Agamemnon*." She suggested that in such a comparison, other things being equal, the length of a

poem must count for something, and that, therefore, the *Iliad* might have a prior claim. He,
however, stuck to his opinion that the *Agamemnon*
is "the grandest work of creative genius in the
whole range of literature," and added that, the
oftener he read it, the more he admired it.

Others of his friends besides Miss Swanwick
had experience of his attempts to break the social
ice by plunging headlong into a discussion. A
very shy young lady, paying him a first visit, was
startled by the question : "Which is your favourite
English sonnet ?" He himself was especially
fond of Wordsworth's sonnet on *Westminster
Bridge*, and of Blanco White's only sonnet. I
am told that he sometimes asked ladies what they
thought of this last sonnet, as a sure test of their
literary judgment. He cared little for *John
Inglesant*. To a lady who inquired whether he
liked it, he gave what in the *Art of Pluck* is called
the *answer indirect :* "You are asking me what
everybody asks me everywhere." I am now
bordering on a province of my subject which I
enter with some trepidation.

"Like all good men," says Mr. Leslie Stephen,
"[Samuel] Johnson loved good women, and liked
to have on hand a flirtation or two, as warm as
might be within the bounds of due decorum." It
is undeniable that this somewhat exclusive test of

goodness would not exclude Pattison, who at times seemed to agree with the hero of *Amours de Voyage*, that *Vir sum, nihil fœminei a me alienum puto*. To speak more seriously, he sought and obtained what has been called the one compensation of growing old. The praise which Wordsworth bestowed on Nature, may more truly be applied to a good woman—she never yet betrayed the heart that loved her; and Pattison stood in special need of that restful sympathy which women know how to give, which good women will give when they feel that it is valued, but which men can neither give nor take away. Yet he learnt by experience that even this rose is not thornless. In particular, he found that the art of instructing and correcting women without affronting them is not easily acquired. The mode of its acquisition, like everything else in which he took an interest, he subjected to critical analysis. "The art of pleasing," I heard him say, "consists in entire self-effacement." This opinion is sanctioned by the high authority of Rochefoucauld (*Maximes*, 139); yet, for all that, it represents only a half-truth. Those who are always taking their own line — whose individuality asserts itself in their own despite — often make the deepest impression on the world. This quality is noticed by Goethe as the chief characteristic of Englishmen:—

c

"Their deportment in society is as full of confidence, and as easy as if they were lords everywhere and the whole world belonged to them.   This it is which pleases our women. . . . They [Englishmen] have the courage to be that for which nature made them. There is nothing vitiated or spoilt about them, there is nothing half-way or crooked ; but, such as they are, they are complete men. That they are also sometimes complete fools, I allow with all my heart ; but that is still something, and has still always some weight in the scale of nature."*

The Rector, however, might fairly have rejoined that, now at any rate, the ordinary John Bull is not a favourite with Germans, and that a few lessons in self-effacement would do him no harm.

I drew Pattison's attention to a statement which he had made in an article in the *Academy*, that " it is difficult to be loved too much by one sex and enough by the other " ; and I asked how he explained the anomaly.   He answered that it is not so much that a lady's man (in the best sense of the term) excites jealousy in other men, but rather that there is something in his temperament by which they are repelled. May not the fact be that all women, except the very best, like " more self-effacement " in men, than men like in each other ? Goethe has noted how hard and important it is in friendship to avoid being either too confidential or

* Eckermann's *Conversations* (Oxenford's translation). Compare Sterne's *Sentimental Journey, Character—Versailles.*

too reserved. The difficulty is closely allied to one pointed out by Horace—to that of hitting the exact mean between *Scurrantis species* and *Asperitas agrestis et inconcinna,* the mean between being hypocritical and hypercritical, or rather between an excessive desire to please and a bluntness which degenerates into brutality. Unfortunately, women, as a rule, like the mean to incline towards the former of these extremes, while men like it to incline towards the latter. In support of this view, I will remark that women are pleased by a man who keeps conversation going, whereas men prefer one who seldom speaks unless he has something to say.

The Rector once reminded me what a different thing it is to understand a subject and to be able to teach it. He said this with special reference to the difficulty of teaching women unofficially. The social superiority of their sex has, as he expressed it, " passé dans les mœurs." And this superiority is wont to clash with the instructor's superiority in age and in knowledge. Female pupils do not receive the moral tonic which is given to male pupils. If they are silly or obstinate, their teacher seldom contradicts them sharply, and never ridicules them. The anomaly of this relation was felt by Pattison all the more, because he had rather strong views as to the intellectual inferiority of the average woman to the average man. Indeed, his love of paradox led him to speak as if he imagined *Ens rationale* to be the definition, not of *Homo*, but of *Vir*. I asked him what he thought of the unchivalrous remark attributed to Disraeli, that all women require flattery : did the author of this remark merely use the word *flattery* as a satirical equivalent to *égards ?* did he merely mean that women receive and expect, in compensation for their weakness, a deferential homage from men not wholly unlike that which a Prime Minister pays to a constitutional Sovereign ? " What Disraeli calls flattery," replied Pattison, " I call economy of truth. I feel that, when I, an old man of seventy, am talking on intellectual subjects to a young girl of seventeen, she and I are on quite different planes of thought ; and it is necessary to translate my ideas into her language. If she talks nonsense, I take refuge in flight. I always agree ; but, when she thinks that her prejudices are quite secure, I slowly try to undermine them." (He emphasized the word *undermine* by moving his out-stretched hand diagonally downwards.)   Of his tendency to self-caricature — of his seeming to take the inverted motto, *Video pejora proboque*, without adding, *Sed meliora sequor* — more will be said presently. I will now merely observe that such

utterances of his as the above are to be taken
cum grano salis, or rather *cum pleno salino.* The
truth which probably underlies his exaggeration is
that, in arguing with women (always excepting
the very best), it is hard for men to maintain the
same perfect frankness, or rather directness, which
they maintain in arguing with each other. The
Rector, so far from being a dissembler or even a
self-effacer, was in reality somewhat over-frank.
He was visited by a young lady who wrote
well, but who in his opinion talked less well. He
resolved to admonish her of this defect; but,
instead of trying in any of the thousand-and-one
possible ways to hint, while commending her
writings, that more was now expected of her dis-
course—*laudando præcipere,* as Bacon would have
said,—he embarrassed her by the blunt rebuke:
" Your conversational utterances are feeble."

The following abridgment of an account which
he gave of his meeting an American young lady
at a foreign *table d'hôte,* reproduces his characteristic sayings almost, if not quite, *verbatim :* " She
was only nineteen, but she knew everything. She
told me the exact amount of affection which the
Princess C. has for her future husband; and she
gave me a full account of the divorce laws in all
the States of America. She appealed to me sometimes; of course I agreed. At last, she asked

whether I did not think she could write a book;
and I told her that she was the most ignorant girl
I ever met! But I took care to say so in such a
way that she couldn't mind it." I doubt not that
in this description the Rector was jocularly over-
stating both the parts which he acted—the part of
assentator and the part of candid friend. Still,
after making allowance for such exaggeration, I
wonder whether in the latter charácter he was quite
as agreeable to the young lady as he imagined.

I asked him whether he agreed with Sainte-Beuve
in thinking that the advice contained in Lord Chesterfield's *Letters* was such as Horace might have
given to his son, if he had had one. The only
answer which I could get from him was, " Horace
would have thought a son a great bore." Yet he
regarded Chesterfield's *Letters* as a repertory of
maxims which might be useful to the social tac-
tician. Indeed, he himself (as we have seen) was
theoretically an adept in *gynæcology*—the science
of womankind. But I doubt his being equally
successful in the practical application of that
science. A lady once complained, " The Rector
treats me like an intellectual machine." And
I suspect that in general, when he had but just
removed the scales from a female pupil's eyes, he
was too apt to shed on her a dry (or rather an
achromatic) light—thought uncoloured by feeling.

On the whole, I am less disposed to think that he was much liked by all, or by most women, than that he was very much liked by a few.

Biography is sometimes autobiography in disguise. The following extract from the *Life of Milton* is obviously founded—indeed, its author admitted that it is founded—more or less on personal experience :—

"Milton longed to be loved that he might love again. But he had to pay the penalty of all who believe in their own ideas, in that their ideas come between them and the persons that approach them, and constitute a mental barrier which can only be broken down by sympathy. And sympathy for ideas is hard to find, just in proportion as those ideas are profound, far reaching, the fruit of long study and meditation. Hence it was that Milton did not associate readily with his contemporaries, but was affable and instructive in conversation with young persons, and those who would approach him in the attitude of disciples."

More than once, when "disciples" were staying with the Rector, he and they together concocted a translation which was sent in for the Prize offered by the *Journal of Education.* I was startled when he told me that one of these joint productions obtained only a 4th Class. At first I conjectured that this was a practical illustration of the maxim Οὐκ ἀγαθὸν πολυκοιρανίη—a mishap, such as often befalls a plurality of generals in the waging of war or a plurality of cooks in the making of broth. But

I found that this explanation would not serve : the Rector assured me that he revised the translation so thoroughly as to make it virtually his own. I was therefore still more amazed when I heard from a sleeping partner, so to say, in the translators' firm, that one of their compositions fell as low as the 7th Class. But my surprise was lessened when my informant added that Pattison's translation was a very free one—so free, indeed, that, finding sentiments or metaphors in the original which were not to his liking, he took upon himself to be wise above that which was written, and to idealise instead of reproducing !*

This masterful mode of translating tallies well with his strong desire that his pupils and friends should always use the best phrases and forms of speech. He protested even against the common error of calling a *sarcastic* smile a *sardonic* one. He and I once talked over the old tradition—a tradition mentioned, I think, by a Scholiast on Homer—from which the word " sardonic " is said to have sprung. In very early times the natives of Sardinia were wont to eat such of their countrymen as were worn out by age. But, as manners grew milder, it was not thought seemly that a patriarch should be thus doomed without his own

---

* Pattison would doubtless have endorsed Moritz Haupt's paradox, " Translation is the death of understanding."

consent; and, in proof that his consent was freely
given, he was himself chosen to bid the guests.
Such, however, was the force of public opinion
(opponents of euthanasia should make a note of
this) that the veteran always issued the invita-
tions to the supper where, in Hamlet's phraseology, he would not eat but be eaten. The courteous
smile which beamed on the old gentleman's countenance as he was doing this last act of hospi-
tality—ἑκὼν ἀέκοντί γε θυμῷ—is the prototype of all
sardonic smiles. For the truth of this ghastly
story the Rector would not vouch; but he insisted
that the word "sardonic" should be used in the
sense which the story indicates. In short, he
wished his pupils to remember that a sardonic
laugh is a laugh at one's own expense, and on the
wrong side of one's mouth. From the following
remarks, it will appear that he himself laughed
sardonically at the world.

The passage chosen as motto for this article
has been severely condemned by Mazzini, and to
many it may appear cynical. But I have chosen
it as putting into a clear light the point of view
from which Pattison should be judged. He once
remarked to me emphatically, " There has only
been one Goethe." Yet, on another occasion, he
protested against the attempts that are often made

to exalt Goethe into a moral hero, and even described him as stamping morality under his feet. This censure is doubtless exaggerated, and indeed was probably not meant to be taken literally. Yet the Rector's judgment of Goethe, both on its favourable and on its unfavourable side, has much in common with the following extract from a famous writer :—

"Chaque ordre de grandeur a sa maîtrise à part et ne doit point être comparé à d'autres. Un philanthrope qui, ayant à juger Goethe, le mettrait en parallèle avec Vincent de Paule, se trouverait amené à ne voir dans le plus grand génie des temps modernes qu'un égoiste qui n'a rien fait pour le bonheur et l'amélioration morale de ses contemporains."*

I quote this passage because Pattison, as well as Goethe, has been accused of moral insensibility. The charge against the Rector is unjust, but not wholly inexplicable. He was, at least in his later years, essentially a scholar, valuing the spread of knowledge more

"Than aught, divine or holy, else enjoyed
    In vision beatific."

The French employ their barely translatable term *l'idéal* to include *le vrai, le beau,* and *le bien.* It would seem that many persons who devote

---

* A similar sentiment is expressed by Mommsen when contrasting the merits of the Romans with those of the Greeks. The passage is quoted in *Safe Studies,* p. 278, Note.

themselves to seeking *l'idéal* through *le beau* or through *le vrai,* have a special difficulty in seeking it through what in the narrower sense may be called *le bien :* in other words, scholars and philo-sophers often lack the enthusiasm of humanity. This is one reason why saints and sages so seldom quite understand one another. Dean Church can as little do justice to Bacon as Bacon could have written the *Life of St. Anselm.*

In order to illustrate further our view of Patti-son's ethical langour, it will be needful to dwell at some length on his scepticism and cynicism. He told me that he objected to auricular confession chiefly because it made people examine themselves too closely. He expressed this opinion in reply to a question as to what he thought of the following sentiment of Goethe :—

"It has at all times been said and repeated that man should strive to know himself. This is a singular requisi-tion, with which no one complies, or indeed ever will comply. . . . I know not myself, and God forbid I should."

How was it that, whereas the greatest moral teacher of antiquity took as his motto, " Know thyself," this great modern teacher virtually said, " Know not thyself " ? Are the two maxims as much opposed to one another as at first sight appears ? The answer probably is that they are not; for, while Socrates addressed his exhorta-

tion to the mass of men, Goethe limited his admonition to the few who are possessed with the
demon of self-consciousness. Our meaning will
be made clearer by an illustration. Aurora Leigh
says, of one whom she elsewhere calls a " good "
man, that

> " He sets his virtues on so raised a shelf,
>   To keep them at the grand millennial height,
>   He has to mount a stool to get at them ;
>   And, meantime, lives on quite the common way,
>   With everybody's morals."

Now, it is plain that, when this " good " man
acquiesced (as almost everyone acquiesces) in the
moral code of those around him, more qualms
would be felt by him than by men whose ideal
was less exalted ; and also that, if he was given
to honest introspection, those qualms might become
very inconvenient. It is indeed possible that, by
fostering this introspection, he would be converted
into a hero. But it is quite as likely that he
would be unfitted for action, would become powerless to prevent the pale cast of his thoughts from
discolouring resolution and enthusiasm—φιλο-
σοφεῖν ἄνευ μαλακίας. The fact seems to be that,
while most good men require the brightest ideals of
character and conduct to light them on the road
to virtue, the too clear sight of some philosophers
is dazzled by the contrast between the brightness

of those ideals and the dark shade of the actual. Cynicism is, as it were, the smoked glass which these latter employ to prevent being dazzled over-much.

We never, says Goethe, feel so much at ease with our own consciences as when we are dwelling complacently on the faults of others. And it is by reason of the restlessness of the intellectual conscience that the intellectual man of the world is tempted to use cynical language, which shocks and startles unintellectual men who are not a bit less worldly than himself.* We thus understand why Talleyrand, being informed of two faults of a lady of his acquaintance, exclaimed, " Elle est détestable, elle n'a que ces deux fautes-là " ; why Disraeli, if rightly reported, censured a Liberal statesman as not having even " a redeeming vice " ; why Goethe maintained that Spinozism, when manipulated by reflection, becomes Machiavellism ; and why Gibbon seems happier when discovering the sins of the good and the follies of the wise, even than when relating the murder of a priest.

It is probable that one cause of the strange

---

* It is my experience that, while most intellectual *men* prefer Thackeray to Dickens, nearly all *women* prefer Dickens to Thackeray. If this is so, is it not because women, being rarely troubled with self-knowledge, have no relish for cynicism ?

repugnance which such men as these feel for heroic virtue, is to be found in their sympathy with those whose welfare has been more or less directly, more or less completely, sacrificed—with the sons of Brutus and the brother of Timoleon. But a more important cause is, that a degree of disinterestedness, of which introspective minds are even too apt to think themselves incapable, is contemplated in others only with pain.

These considerations are meant to explain, not to justify, the ordinary type of cynicism. They must be pushed somewhat further to cover the case of Pattison. A distinguished pupil of his assures me that, at the time of the Tractarian movement, he had a high spiritual ideal, that he lost that ideal when he changed his views, and that he keenly felt the loss of it.* At this crisis of his life, he had much in common with the exiled Psalmist, whose affections would not take root in a strange country, and who looked wistfully back on the days when *Stantes erant pedes*

---

* This paragraph had been written before I had read the *Memoirs;* I leave it in its original form as an independent testimony. To Pattison may be applied some of Macaulay's remarks about Shrewsbury, who, after a long and painful struggle, shook off the yoke of his early Catholic training: "The shock which had overturned his early prejudices had at the same time unfixed all his opinions" [and some of his principles].—*History*, Vol. II., p. 128, ed. 1866.

nostri in atriis tuis, Jerusalem. To the typical scholar of our generation may be applied the words of its typical poet :—

> " Of all the creatures under heaven's wide cope,
>   We are most hopeless, who had once most hope,
>   And most beliefless, that had most believed."

It is not impossible that the line preceding these,

> " Eat, drink, or die, for we are souls bereaved,"

would express the despairing state into which he fell. A great writer has remarked that we feel what our ancestors thought, and that posterity will feel what we think. May not much of the spiritual anguish of our generation be due to the fact that many of us think with philosophers, while feeling with theologians ? It was perhaps through being in this condition that Pattison continued long in the Slough of Despond. There is even reason to fear that, for some years, the loss of the ideal had on him a natural but melancholy effect, similar to that which (in the fable) the loss of the tail had on the fox. It is, however, right to mention that his mental struggles affected his nerves, and that these reacted on his mental condition. Speaking of his state at this time, my friend writes :

> " What his physical condition was then,—without being ill,—may be judged from one fact. He most kindly gave

me a private lecture in *Magna Charta;* we both adopted the position of seekers. During an animated discussion of Hallam's views, I turned aside to collate some reading. On looking round, Pattison was fast asleep; and this is how he often seemed in those years, wearied out with vexations, and as if he might sink into an exhausted sleep at any moment."

It should also be stated that my informant was intimate with Pattison chiefly when he was smarting under a sense of grievous injustice after the failure of his first candidature for the Rectorship; and it is thought that haply, for some years, the loss of his ideal and the loss of his election combined to give bitterness to his conversation. This is important as throwing light both on the origin and on the original form of his cynicism. But, when I knew him, his state of mind was different. I never detected in him the least resemblance to the *esprit fort* (or *faible*) who exclaimed : "Lord, I cannot believe; help thou mine unbelief." His cynicism seemed to me to be the outcome of deliberate reason, and to have become a second nature to him: and as such I shall attempt to describe it.

"It is not desirable," says Bagehot, "to take this world too much *au sérieux;* most persons will not; and the one in a thousand who will, should not." In other words, a man of that abnormal type ought to make a conscious effort, if not to become what the French call a *farceur,* and what Bacon in his essay on *Fortune* calls *poco di matto*, at least to avoid being righteous over-much, and being over-wise. This was just the sort of exhortation which Pattison needed, which he knew that he needed, and which he tried, not very successfully, to follow : he was, as it were, an *homme sérieux malgré lui*.

If I were asked to what he owed this peculiarity of temperament, I should say that it was partly due to his retentiveness of memory, or rather to his inability to forget. Darwin, in explaining the genesis of morals among primitive men, attributes much to the influence of memory. When the best of our early ancestors saw a neighbour suffering, they were haunted by the recollection of what they themselves had suffered. When they were tempted to do wrong, they could not always banish the thought of their own resentment when injured. This *importunateness* of memory, arising under different conditions and associated (as it often is) with nervous weakness, contributes much both to the merits and to the defects of such men as the Rector : they cannot get rid of their former selves. Of the many illustrations of my meaning, the most obvious must suffice. When a man labours to avert or to postpone a change which he regards as hurtful or premature, it is hardly possible for him to avoid exaggerating the evils of that change, and thus becoming an alarmist. When another or the same man seeks to evolve the energy needful for carrying out some great reform or establishing a scientific truth, it is perhaps impossible for him to avoid greatly exaggerating the importance of his undertaking, and thus becoming a strong optimist. It is through this and other causes that nearly every one of us oscillates between a modified pessimism (or at least uneasiness about the future) and a decided optimism; and during these oscillations an ordinary Philistine, however strong his affirmations may be on either side, has an enviable faculty of believing in himself. To Pattison and his peers this convenient self-deception is impossible. Their Liberal zeal is checked by the unwelcome memory of their fits of pessimism, and their Conservative zeal by the memory of their fits of optimism. No doubt, they are thus preserved from much extravagance; but they tend, in the phraseology of Burns, to become "tideless blooded." This word exactly expresses Pattison's chief fault, or rather his *misfortune;* for it was his misfortune that states of feeling which appear to ordinary men as a series of dissolving views, each distinct in itself, blended themselves before his mind's-eye and made a sort of blur.* Renan has said, "Presque tous nous sommes doubles," and has somewhere maintained the paradox : "Woe to the man who does not contradict himself at least once a day."† In a like spirit, Pattison, when reminded that some principle or policy which he was upholding was opposed to principles laid down in his writings, used to exclaim jestingly, "It is more than five minutes ago that I wrote that," or again, "Who ever dreamt of reconciling practice and theory ?" Yet, while thus professing indifference, he was really anxious, perhaps over-anxious, to see practice and theory fitting one another like hand and glove. To quote again from the writer who so well illustrates this subject : "The man," says Goethe, "who would do all that is expected of him, must overrate himself a little—perhaps more

* Since writing this, I have learnt that he once quoted the following passage (from Lewes's *Life of Goethe*) in explanation of his own character : "There is in men of active intellects, and especially in men of imaginative, apprehensive intellects, a fluctuation of motives keeping the volition in abeyance, which practically amounts to weakness. This is the weakness of imaginative men." This reminds one of Macaulay's character of Halifax.

† Mr. Maurice notes "one important quality of Boswell. He never stumbled at contradictions. Johnson often said things directly inconsistent with each other. Most thoughtful men who speak what they mean, and feel strongly at any given time, do."

than a little, if he thinks about himself at all."
And, on the other hand, he who dwells constantly
on the seamy side of his own work, needs to be
reminded that there is just as seamy a side to the
work of others, or he will think himself the worst
sempster in the world.   In the phrase of the
eminent Oxonian who is now, as he was thirty
years ago, the greatest teacher in the University,
such a man is too much "under the dominion of
logic."   Pattison was under that dominion; and,
when logical power, mnemonic power, and nervous weakness are combined as they were in
him, they indicate a person to whom, not indeed
pecca fortiter, but μάθε παίζειν would be wholesome
advice :

> "amara lento
> Temperet risu; nihil est ab omni
> Parte beatum."

Such a man as we have described could hardly
fail to be given to paradoxes; and, in fact, as we
have already intimated, Pattison revelled in them.
Sometimes he was paradoxically sceptical.   I once
asked him whether it is not certain that we owe
much to the Catholic Church for the wisdom with
which in the Middle Ages she insisted on the
celibacy of the priests, as the only means of
securing their independence of the barons.   "We
always say so," was his characteristic rejoinder,

" but I don't know on what evidence." On one occasion, his paradoxical temper found vent in an anti-Liberal ebullition worthy of Carlyle:—" I should like to see the anniversary of the day on which Cromwell closed the door of the House of Commons kept as the greatest day of our calendar." This, however, seems to have represented a passing phase of his opinions; for I am assured that he sometimes defended constitutional government as the least unsatisfactory of all forms of government. I once discussed with him the singular superiority, in point of ability, of the Liberal to the Conservative party in the House of Commons. " Yes," he observed, " the best thing about parliamentary government is that it tends to bring the ablest men to the front."

I spoke to him about the last patriarch of Benthamism, Mr. George Norman, who, like his friend, Mr. Grote, inclined to Conservatism in his old age. Mr. Norman once said to me, " I only wish that Gladstone would leave us without organic changes for the next forty years " (a sentiment which sounds very like " Après moi *et mon fils* le déluge "): and, on another occasion, he made the gloomy prediction : " Sooner or later, there must be a struggle between *those who have got* and *those who want*, and I don't see how it is to be settled except by the sword. But I suppose that *those who have got* will win." "True," said Pattison, when this augury of ill was repeated to him; "in the end *those who have got* will win. But, in the meantime, everything will have been lost which had been gained during the half-century before; and, soon after the civil strife is settled, it will be ready to break out again."

The halting attitude which he was wont to assume when confronted by wide generalizations, may be illustrated by his view of the great principle that representation ought to be coextensive with taxation. It is plain that, as every one, directly or indirectly, pays taxes, the principle, pressed to its extreme conclusions, would give manhood and womanhood, if not what may be termed *childhood*, suffrage to every inhabitant, civilized or uncivilized, of our entire Indian and Colonial empire; and that it would lead to the parcelling out of the empire into equal electoral districts. It will doubtless be objected that the franchise should not be given to incompetent persons. But, in truth, this qualification is an all-important one. That, in strict theory, the franchise ought to be given to every taxpayer, but that, in practice, it should be withheld from unfit persons, and *that the present holders of power are to be judges of their unfitness,*—this is a principle to which the highest Tory need not demur.

After we had touched on these points, Pattison said thoughtfully : " In fact, it comes to this,— the principle will not bear examination." Nevertheless, he doubtless thought that the old Whigs acted wisely in assuming the correctness of this exaggerated ideal as a basis for carrying the Reform Bill, and that future reformers will have to follow their example. Indeed, he approvingly quoted an Aristotelian maxim to the effect that, when we would obtain a little from mankind, it is often needful to ask for a great deal.

He brought a like spirit to bear on the question of nationality. " The age of patriotism," he said, " is passing away, and the age of cosmopolitanism is taking its place." Irish Home Rule was not to his liking ; and he regarded the cry " Egypt for the Egyptians " as, if not a *reductio ad absurdum*, at least a natural sequel of the cry " Ireland for the Irish." On my asking whether he was not of opinion that the Irish Land Bill was opposed to the principles of political economy, as those principles used to be commonly understood, he interrupted me by saying, " Of course, it is confiscation." Yet he was not prepared to deny that, in the present state of public opinion, the Bill was inevitable. It should be added that he regretted the sympathy shown by some Oxford Liberals for Lord Beaconfield's foreign policy.

In a word, he was a Whig, and not a Jingo.

It may be instructive to observe that between Pattison and Charles Austin there were many points of comparison and a few of contrast. The chief difference between them was, that Pattison had far less political and patriotic enthusiasm than Austin had. Austin (as his brother told me), shortly before he died, went to a public meeting at St. James's Hall, where the band suddenly struck up the *Marseillaise*. He had long since laid aside his juvenile sympathy with the French Revolution; yet, on hearing the old familiar strain, he rose from his seat (old and infirm as he was), and the tears came to his eyes. Personally I never saw him thus give way to his feelings; but I remember his saying that he pitied the man whose spirit was not stirred by the cry for deliverance in the *Persæ* :—

Ὦ παῖδες Ἑλλήνων, ἴτε,
ἐλευθεροῦτε πατρίδ', ἐλευθεροῦτε δὲ
παῖδας, γυναῖκας, θεῶν τε πατρῴων ἕδη.

Pattison, so far as I could judge, had hardly a spark of this patriotic zeal. His want of interest in the politics of the day is well shown by a habit of his, which is reported to me at first hand. He never turned to the newspapers till 9 p.m., and then chiefly from a sense of duty.* Generally, instead of reading them himself, he would lie down on his sofa, take out his watch, and shut his eyes, while his niece looked down the columns, and gave him the shortest possible epitome of the *Times.* If she got through it in less than twenty minutes, she was commended. But he liked to hear, at least, the heading of everything; and, if any event was afterwards mentioned which she had overlooked, he would say reproachfully, "I suppose that was not in our copy."

We once talked over the romantic visit paid to Greece by the statesman whom the Greeks called ὁ φιλέλλην καὶ περίφημος Γλάδστων. In the conversation, a passage from the Acharnians was applied to the visit—

Περικλέης οὐλύμπιος
ἤστραπτεν, ἐβρόντα, ξυνεκύκα τὴν Ἑλλάδα.

Pattison seemed pleased with the quotation, and begged to hear it again. In referring to the modern Pericles (scholar, orator, reformer), he acknowledged that he had little sympathy with him; adding, "It is strange that he is the living representative of the Liberal cause, the cause of

* He told a friend that he did not like to have the news "hot"—he preferred giving it time to cool. According to Goethe, you may often with advantage delay reading newspapers, as to-morrow's news may correct to-day's.

wisdom and righteousness throughout all time."
On my asking whether some share of the credit
was not due to the Conservative party on the
ground that it *cunctando restituit rem*, he merely
answered, " Sir Stafford Northcote is the representative of everything which distinguishes Englishmen from Americans." This damning with
faint praise may prepare my readers for his having
said, in his half-jesting way, " Though I am
always abusing the Liberals, I call myself a
Liberal, *and I am one*." He expressed his regret
at the death of the Prince Consort by saying that
it was as great a misfortune as a ten-years'
innings of the Conservative party. He was told
of a very lukewarm Liberal who said that, so far
as the society is concerned, he would rather belong
to the Carlton than to the Reform Club. " He is quite
right," said the Rector; " Reformers are generally so rough and rude. Of course, the Whigs of
Holland House were exceptions. But, as a general
rule, my advice is *to live with the Tories and to vote
with the Whigs*." A cynic might add that those
who purpose following this advice, would be wise
in taking full advantage of the Ballot, and not
letting their High Tory friends suspect that they
vote against them.

His Liberalism did not incline him to what is
called the Birmingham School. In reference to

an eminent writer and editor who has become a strong Radical, he said: "He has taken so much pains about *l'art d'écrire*, that he has not left himself time to acquire *l'art de vivre*. The two arts are very different, and the one often unfits a man for the other." I asked him whether De Tocqueville had not stated too broadly that the advent of democracy was inevitable. "Since he died," answered the Rector, "everything seems to be fulfilling his predictions. Nothing can stop the movement. The more you give the people, the more they will want." I called his attention to an assertion of Mr. Herbert Spencer to the effect, that the time will come when one man will not be suffered to enjoy, without working, that which another man works for without enjoying; and I asked him whether such a state of public opinion would not exclude domestic service, and, indeed, all social inequalities. "I fear it must be so," he replied. "Everything seems to be tending towards Socialism. *I hate it.*" I asked why, if so great an evil is approaching, he and those who think with him do not try to stop it. "Look there," he said, pointing to the sea at Biarritz. "Just as men can construct moles and breakwaters against the waves, so individuals can, in some slight degree, modify passing events. They are as powerless against the tide of history, as they are against the tide of the ocean. No ; what is to be, will be, in spite of you and me."

It may be well to insert the epitome of a conversation which sets forth the Rector's manner of dealing with this subject, though it shows him in an unusual attitude — an attitude of defence. I reminded him that in one of his writings he had expressed a view (seemingly shared by Hallam) that Englishmen were, on the whole, better off in the reign of George II. than either before or since. He told me that he had been taken to task for this assertion, but he seemed prepared to defend it, and also to predict that England would go on declining. I insisted that, in discussing the question, we must start with the assumption that there is more good than evil in life. " I don't see," he exclaimed, " why I should assume anything of the sort; I think I shall take up the view of Schopenhauer." I recalled to him some of the conclusions that may be drawn from that wildly anti-social theory—such conclusions, for instance, as the following : Ought not these very numerous persons who say that they would not, if they could, live their lives over again—in other words, that, so far as their experience goes, the good of life is a *minus* quantity,—ought not these Schopenhauerites to rejoice instead of sorrowing at the sight or news of a shipwreck ? " Well," he

said, " suppose I grant that life is a good, what
has that to say to human progress ? " " For con-
venience of figures," I answered, "let us compare the present time with a time when the population of England was one-third of what it now is,
and let us suppose that the average Englishman
was twice as happy as now—even on this extreme
supposition, the aggregate of happiness in England
would be half as great again now as then ; Englishmen, in tripling their numbers, would have gained
more collectively than they have lost individually."
" Yes, yes," he said, with amused impatience,
" but this is not what is generally meant by progress." I never could draw him further than this
on the optimistic path. Indeed, he seemed generally half to expect, as the most eminent of
French critics half expects,* that, when reformers
have done their perfect work, the world, destitute
of variety and originality, will become a sort of
universal China — a lubberland of lotos-eaters.
Nor could he fail to see the inferences that might
be drawn from such a prognostication. A great
living philologist has expressed the opinion that
the classical languages and literatures paid for
their temporary splendour by their premature

---

* Scherer—*Etudes*, Vol. v. pp. 316, 317 (on Renan), and
Vol vii. p. 64 (on Carlyle).

decay. If it is likewise true that all civilization tends to decay, analogy might warrant the conjecture that patriotic and philanthropic zealots are, so to say, making the world live its life too fast, and hurrying it on to its senile decrepitude. If so, it is not a mere *counsel of imperfection* fitted for men of the world, a mere concession to the hardness of their hearts, but the highest Utilitarian ideal, that is embodied in the suggestion of the most philosophical of our judges, that perhaps " the respectable man . . . who led an easy life will turn out to have been right after all, and enthusiastic believers of all creeds to have been quite wrong." I enunciate this violent paradox, not as expressing the settled convictions of any one, but as furnishing a sample of a class of doubts which, more or less consciously, present themselves to men like Pattison, and effectually deprive them, if not of the enthusiasm of humanity, at least of what may be termed the enthusiasm of progress.

We have before stated that Pattison was not, as indeed no one can be, a consistent pessimist. By urging on education and other reforms, he showed that he was practically a believer in progress. Yet, even as a believer in progress, he was perplexed by ethical puzzles which differ from the pessimistic ones, but are hardly less embarrassing. He was amused or troubled—amused as the only alternative of being troubled—by such ἀπορίαι as the following : Would not an ideal philanthropist allow himself only the minimum of relaxation that might be necessary for the greatest efficiency of his work ? Would he not sell his gold watch and take third-class railway tickets, so as to have more money to spare for the Anti-Mendicity Society and the Cancer Hospital ? Ought not the passionate lover, before putting the momentous question, to satisfy himself, not merely that he has the means to support a family, but also that the population of the world stands in need of an increase ? Ought we not, when ill, to forsake the medical Philistine who would treat us simply with a view to our own cure, and to resort to the nobler practitioner who would experiment on us for the good of posterity ? To this last question, Pattison laughingly objected that the " neighbour " whom we are commanded to love as ourselves, cannot mean the unborn ; but he knew full well that to laugh was not to solve the riddle. He knew also that these difficulties are increased (or nullified) by a further one, which may be regarded as a phase of *pessimism*, though it represents a novel aspect of that Protean creed. Mill insists that the Utilitarian principle should be applied, not to man only, but to the entire sentient.

universe; and certainly it is less easy to show that
the principle ought not to be so extended, than
that, if so extended, it might involve a *reductio ad
euthanasiam*. May it not be argued that, from
the philozoic point of view, the existence of the
human race is altogether a mishap? Does the
Unconstitutional Monarchy of Man minister to
"the greatest happiness of the greatest number"
of sentient beings (including earwigs and animal-
cules)? "I never could see," said the Rector,
when dealing seriously with such questions, "any
way of disposing of extreme cases, except by
taking the matter at the other end, and asking:
*What reason can you allege for the obligation of
self-sacrifice?*" Perhaps it was in consequence
of this fundamental doubt that he disliked, as he
informed me, to label himself a Utilitarian. His
friend, Henry Smith, told me that he also demurred
to the designation, and for a similar reason. But,
after all, the question is one of words. Charles
Austin, the Utilitarian *par excellence*, sometimes
avowed a logical scepticism as complete as Pattison's; more often, he expressed an opinion different in appearance, but substantially the same.
Goethe has observed that a universal scepticism
always takes refuge in a qualified belief. And
thus there was, in fact, a latent scepticism in a
remark which Austin once made: "I know of no

olbiometer : so we must take the conventional estimate of what leads to pleasure or pain."* In other words, we must not be too logical, but must acquiesce in the moral standard of the good men and women among whom we live. This, I repeat, was Pattison's view; and, if I describe his ethical creed as Utilitarianism tempered by Pyrrhonism, I must be understood to mean no more than this. After all, if he was wrong, he was kept in countenance by the virtuous, nay, over-scrupulous poet who was remarkable for what Bagehot has called a " pleasant cynicism," and who gave a cynical turn even to such pathetic self-revelations as *Dipsychus, Amours de Voyage,* and *In the Great Metropolis.* Mr. Jowett, too, in his strictures on Casuistry, adopts a view similar to that of the best of the *Questioned Spirits,* the Spirit who cut ethical knots by exclaiming,

" I know not, I will do my duty " ;

and whose note was at times saddened into

" I know not, I must do as other men are doing."

---

* A similar view is very strongly expressed by Scherer, in *Etudes,* vi., p. 213 (on Sterne), and in the introduction to Amiel's *Journal,* pp. lxvi., lxvii. (" La vie exige des ménagements, j'allais dire des ruses. . . . . L'art de vivre, c'est de se faire une raison, de souscrire aux compromis, de se prêter aux fictions. . . . . La vie ne supporte pas d'être serrée de [tout] près. C'est une croûte mince sur laquelle il faut

E

The application of this principle may be shown by an example. " Pattison," writes one who knew him well, " was very fond of fishing, but he had grave misgivings as to the moral character of the amusement. He confessed to these, but I do not know that he allowed them to interfere with his practice." Likewise, Austin doubted the morality of field sports, and yet he preserved game for his guests. It is probable that both of these philosophers were acting against what may be termed their logical conscience ; but they were not, in any ordinary sense of the word, *unconscientious*. The worst that can be said about them is, that they were of the marble of which sages are made, but not of the gold of which saints are made. Might they not have contended that they were merely conforming to a custom likely to be considered barbarous by a remote posterity, and that, if we would conform to no custom likely to be so regarded, we (in St. Paul's phrase) " must needs go out of the world " ? *

It will now be understood what I meant when I represented the Rector's cynicism as wholly unlike the vulgar cynicism of less analytical minds.

marcher sans appuyer ; donner du talon dedans, vous ferez un trou où vous disparaîtrez.")

* My view is further illustrated in *Safe Studies*, pp. 230 —234. See also p. 287, note.

From the premise, *Omnia exeunt in absurdum*, he drew the conclusion, *Omnia vanitas.* He feared moral and religious enthusiasm, for he knew not whither it might lead. In the "Memoirs" he remarks quaintly—very quaintly for a clergyman —that "Religion is a good servant, but a bad master," which is the exact equivalent of Goethe's famous aphorism : "Religion is not an end, but a means, to lead us through the purest tranquillity of mind to the highest culture." In like manner, he felt that *Imperat aut servit recti mens conscia cuique.* He was (to use his own phrase) " haunted by the ideal, and baffled by philosophical perplexities,"—haunted and baffled all the more painfully, because others, far inferior to him in intellect, rose, through being unweighted by those perplexities, to a somewhat Pharisaical ideal—because they, not having tasted of the Tree of Knowledge, ate and condemned him for not eating of the Tree of Life. This being duly considered, it will be found that his sceptical, caustic, and jaunty sayings generally leave in the mouth no taste save that of a tonic bitter. We may, therefore, without scruple, give a few more examples of the cynicism which so belonged to him that one almost missed it if ever he laid it aside.

We will begin with an aphorism of his which may have been suggested by Mill's well-known statement that in England the upper classes for the most part do not lie, and that the lower classes, though almost habitually liars, are generally ashamed of lying. "Englishmen," said Pattison, "lie as much as foreigners; but Englishmen have a dim consciousness that they are lying, while foreigners believe all the while that they are telling the truth." This preferring of conscious guilt to guilt born of self-deceit, will at once recall Aristotle's comparison between ἀκρασία and ἀκολασία, and perhaps is not wholly unlike St. Paul's comparison between doing wrong things and having pleasure in them that do them. I remember asking Charles Austin if he did not think that too much fuss was made when a late Bishop of Durham appointed a highly respectable son-in-law to a good living. Being in a paradoxical vein, he answered: "What I mind is, not the thing that was done, but the sanctimonious way in which it was done. If Ben Stanley had done anything of the kind, he would have written in big letters in his diary, *This is a job*, and that would not have been half as bad. I should not hate Torquemada so much if I did not know that he was thoroughly convinced that he was doing his duty." Carlyle has paid Frederic the equivocal compliment that, although he often deceived others, he never deceived himself.

Pattison was coaching an undergraduate in the *Ethics*. The pupil, perplexed by Aristotle's reasoning, embarrassed his teacher by his importunate desire to understand it. At last Pattison said tartly: "Never mind understanding it, only get it up." The pupil was naturally hurt by this unpleasant rebuke; which, however, probably meant that the time was short, and that, if the pupil insisted on discussing first principles, instead of merely learning the answers which would satisfy the examiners, he might be disappointed in his degree, as Pattison himself had been. Nevertheless, Pattison's impatience may have been partly due to want of sympathy with the subject. When I knew him, and when he wrote his *Memoirs*, he was an Aristotelian. But he was originally a Platonist, and it was only by slow degrees that the influence of Oxford wrought the change in him. Many years ago, when speaking of the late Dr. Jeune as a successful man of the world whom he disliked, he said, " I divide men into those who love Plato and those who do not; Jeune, I am certain, does not."

When a new edition of Shakespeare came out, he said to a friend, " Instead of bringing out these old plays, why don't the editors write new ones ?" My informant understood him to mean that the prevalent Shakespearolatry is a mere delusion. If he really held this opinion, he had given it up when he wrote his *Life of Milton*, and when I knew him. He told me, however, that he thought that there is much exaggeration in the popular judgment on the subject, and that the great excellence of Shakespeare is to be sought in the beautiful passages that abound in his plays, rather than in his power of delineating character. He took greater delight in reading the Sonnets than the Plays; he found fault with *Romeo and Juliet*, and even *The Tempest* was not one of his favourites. Every old man, says Goethe, is a King Lear. It is characteristic of Pattison that he regarded *King Lear* and *Père Goriot* as superior in tragic interest to any other modern works of fiction.

He certainly used odd language about poets. In an article on Tennyson, I had contrasted the poet with more mature thinkers. Pattison wrote to me: "The phrase, 'more mature thinkers,' implies that Tennyson is a thinker at all. Is he so? Is he not a poet, and are not poets and thinkers incompatibles?" This can only have meant that a poet, *quâ* poet, is not a thinker, and that it would go hardly even with the greatest poets if we subjected their reasoning to the severe test which we apply to the reasoning of philosophers. Hamlet's soliloquy assuredly could not bear that test.

" The religion of uneducated [unphilosophical] persons is the same everywhere, and has been the same since the foundation of the world." This oracular sentence was addressed by Pattison to a brother clergyman who, though a Broad Churchman, was rather shocked by it. Its meaning (so far as it has any) probably resembles that of Charles Austin's favourite quotation—the line in which the Tory and orthodox Dryden affirms that " priests of all religion are the same."

One is sometimes startled, after knowing one corner of a great man's mind well, to find how many corners there are of which one knew nothing. In my intercourse with Pattison, I never suspected that he took an interest in otter-hunting and horse-racing. The latter taste is well illustrated by the following anecdote, communicated to me by one of his pupils :—

" The year of the great match between *Voltigeur* and *Flying Dutchman*, he suddenly asked me, which horse would win. I answered calmly : ' It depends on the state of the ground ; the *Dutchman* is the faster horse, but, if the ground is heavy, *Voltigeur* will win.' He seemed delighted with such an answer from a ' slow ' man, but the question followed, ' How did you learn that ?' ' Oh, I talked it over with the coachman on the box as I came up,' and his countenance fell."

During his lifetime I never dreamt that his proficiency in croquet was such that he aspired to become Champion of all England. But I knew that he took an interest in the game. This came out in an odd way. On my mentioning the name of a lady who is a strong advocate of Women's Rights, he exclaimed eagerly, "I know something of Miss ———. She was playing at croquet, and I was acting as head of the side. When it was her turn, I told her not to try to go through the hoop, but merely to place her ball in front of it. She replied stiffly, 'Thank you, I would rather play my own game.' She tried to go through the hoop, missed it, and the game was lost. I said to myself, *That girl has an undisciplined mind.*"

One evening, the Rector, as he was wishing me good-night, told me rather mysteriously that he was going the next day to call on the Editor of the *Times* (Mr. Chenery). I asked whether he thought him an able man. Not being in a communicative mood, he answered, "Do you know that you are putting a very hard question? It is just as if you asked me—well—whether I think Jupiter clever," and he laughed as he hurried away.

He liked novel reading, and it was a sort of affectation with him to seem to like it a great deal (as might perhaps have been inferred from the last sentence in the *Life of Milton*). Being asked whether a former pupil, who was making his mark in the world, kept up his taste for literature, he answered, " Yes, he reads all the novels that come out, *and he remembers them too.*" He declared (how seriously I know not) that he preferred contemporary French literature (including novels) to contemporary English literature. Nor was this the only respect in which he was wont to depreciate the intellectual atmosphere of England. A friend writes :—

" He spoke once somewhat bitterly of the treatment of public men, and men of energy, in England. He said, 'If a man was a country squire and did nothing, just lived an easy, good-tempered sportsman's life, all men spoke well of him, and he was popular, and life was made pleasant for him; immediately a man showed energy and worked, he was thwarted, calumny begun, and he became unpopular. It was so with statesmen, and so with the Bishops. The Bishops who did nothing were liked; Wilberforce (then of Oxford, about 1849-50), who showed some energy, was calumniated and hated by many, and anything was believed against him.' "

Was Pattison also thinking of the contrast between the French admiration for Richelieu and the English abhorrence of Strafford ?

A trifling incident may show how strong was his antipathy to the narrow classical instruction which used to form the chief staple of our public school education. I had been talking about my own school-time at Harrow. He turned round and asked abruptly, "Did you learn anything there?" I hesitated. "Answer me, *Yes* or *No*. Can you recall a single thing worth remembering that you learnt during all the years that you spent there?" I replied that, owing to my extreme short sight and consequent slowness in looking out words in a dictionary, I was not a good sample of a Harrow boy, but that some of my schoolfellows certainly learnt much. "Yes," he said, doubtfully, " perhaps you may be right."

He upbraided me in a sort of semi-banter, because in the *Fortnightly Review* I praised Charles Austin for continuing, when failing health drove him from the Bar, to do what active work he could as Chairman of Quarter Sessions. " Do you know, I feel quite hurt by your saying this? Can you seriously mean that the βίος πρακτικός is superior to the βίος θεωρητικός? I can hardly conceive anything more dreadful than for such a man as Austin to have wasted his time over the drudgery of Quarter Sessions." This is pitched in the same key as the opinion of Goethe, quoted both by Hayward and by Pattison, that " a purely poetical subject is as superior to a political one, as the pure everlasting truth of Nature is to party spirit."

I called the Rector's attention to a very Pattisonian confession of Sainte-Beuve, who seemed to limit his moral aspirations to "un composé de bonnes habitudes, de bonnes manières, d'honnêtes procédés, reposant d'ordinaire sur un fonds plus ou moins généreux, sur une nature plus ou moins bien née;" and I asked him whether the last two words mean *well constituted* (in the sense which Mr. Galton deems so important) or *well-born* (as opposed to *risen from the ranks*). He answered that the latter was the meaning; and, after mentioning a very distinguished self-made man (lately deceased), he put the query, "Could anything have turned him into a gentleman?"

After he had delivered his lecture at Bedford College in 1883, I suggested that he should send it to a new and struggling periodical with which I knew that he warmly sympathized. He answered that the application had already been made by the editor: "It was asking me to make him a present of £25, to which my μεγαλοπρέπεια was not equal. I know I ought to be content with the approval of the Dean of St. Paul's, who wrote to me, 'Nothing so true and so real has been said for a long time'; but I also remember the text, Εἰ ἐν τῷ ἀδίκῳ μαμμωνᾷ πιστοὶ οὐκ ἐγένεσθε, τὸ ἀληθινὸν τίς ὑμῖν πιστεύσει;" He therefore intended to send the revised lecture to a popular magazine, but his intention seems to have been relinquished through failing health. This sounds very mercenary; but, if he had not been a ἑαυτὸν τιμωρούμενος and a ἑαυτοῦ κατηγορῶν, he would have said, and with substantial truth, that his reason for declining the request was a desire to exert an influence over the greatest possible number of readers. I do not blame him for thus writing to me in the cynical dialect, as he knew that I should translate his words into the vernacular. But it is certainly unfortunate that he often used the same dialect, a dialect very open to misconstruction, in addressing persons almost certain to misconstrue it.

A former pupil of Pattison, an orthodox divine, who, though very well off, continues to take an active part in education, told me that the Rector once said to him,—" You are the most ungrateful man in the world. Providence has given you the opportunity of being idle, and you won't take advantage of it." I am sorry that I never asked Pattison whether, in giving this most uncharacteristic advice, he was not thinking of Gibbon's paradox that the vices of the clergy are less dangerous than their virtues—whether, in fact, he was not resorting to an " economy of truth " in the hope of inducing his very ecclesiastical friend to leave education alone. If this was not his meaning, the admonition must have been one of those *counsels of imperfection* to which I have alluded. It is simply impossible that the advice to seek delights and shun laborious days would be given by the censor who has denounced the entire generation of middle-aged Oxford dons as stricken with intellectual palsy. His state of mind was, perhaps, similar to Renan's : " Tout en étant fort appliqué, je me demande sans cesse si ce ne sont pas les gens frivoles qui ont raison." I call attention to this passage, as it is about as good an example as could be given of that *importunateness* of memory and refleciton which is (so to say) the presiding demon of analytical thought.

The gospel of idleness is merely a part of the gospel of self-indulgence ; and the grain of salt which is needed to make the former gospel palatable, or even tolerable, must now be added for the seasoning of the latter. If the following saying of Pattison, the most cynical that I shall quote, can be more or less satisfactorily interpreted, all his cynical sayings can be so interpreted. In *Safe Studies*, p. 187, I enunciate the truism that husband and wife should comfort and sustain one another in struggling for the good of all men. In page 116, I quote with disapproval a strange assertion of Montaigne, " He who abandons his own healthful and pleasant life to serve others, takes, in my opinion, a course that is wrong and unnatural." Concerning these contradictory maxims Pattison wrote : " In page 187, will you

stand to the words 'for the good of all men'?
Do you not much rather incline to endorse Montaigne's opinion, p. 116, a refreshing passage, to
which I wish I had the reference in the original?"
In this frank avowal we seem to hear an echo of
the " Unjust Voice " in the *Clouds* :—

Σκέψαι γὰρ, ὦ μειράκιον, ἐν τῷ σωφρονεῖν ἅπαντα
Ἄνεστιν, ἡδονῶν θ' ὅσων μέλλεις ἀποστερεῖσθαι,
Παίδων, γυναικῶν, κοττάβων, ὄψων, πότων, κιχλισμῶν.
Καίτοι τί σοι ζῆν ἄξιον, τούτων ἐὰν στερηθῇς ;
Neph. 1071—5.

But, on the other hand, Pattison was often on
the side of the *Just Voice*, sometimes in an extreme degree. I remember pleading for that
modified eccentricity, that social independence,
which was so dear to the heart of Mill. Pattison,
himself not the most conventional of men,* surprised me by objecting, "Eccentricity seems to
me a form of egoism, and all egoism ought to
be discouraged." This little sermon of his may
help us to draw the sting from his Apology for
Montaigne. Let us observe that in that Apology
he uses the word " refreshing," which shows that

* For example: after he had only once met Miss Swanwick, he (having, I suppose, chanced to dine in the neigh-
bourhood) sent up his card one evening between 9 and 10,
and asked if she could receive him. She was glad to avail
herself of the opportunity to renew their classical discussions,
but was amused at the hour chosen by her untimely guest.

he stood in need of refreshment—that, in fact he relished Montaigne's aphorism as an anodyne under an oppressive sense of the social martyrdom to which ethical logic might lead. In practice, no doubt, he would have differed from Mill in assigning the limits of self-sacrifice; but, theoretically, his paradoxical words *perhaps* mean no more than Mill would have expressed by saying that, in our present low state of civilization, we cannot ignore the necessity of loving ourselves and those near to us better than those more remote. They *certainly* mean no more than Professor Bain (on *The Study of Character*) has expressed by saying that disinterestedness is "an exception to the only sane principle of conduct, which is, for every being to look to its own pleasures and pains—a brilliant exception, it is true, something of the *splendide mendax*, but never to be made the rule without even suicidal consequences."

We may sum up our view of the Rector's cynicism by affirming that he

"laughed that any one should weep
In this disjointed world for one wrong more."

Or, more shortly, we may say of him, as of Democritus, that he laughed to prevent weeping. Mr. Greg has quaintly remarked that *hardly any one* can afford to keep a conscience, that is, a strictly logical one. He might have maintained that *no one* can afford such a luxury. Clough, whose poetry the Rector (strange to say) did not appreciate, puts the case yet more strongly :—

> " We cannot act without assuming x,
>   And at the same time y, its contradictory;
>   *Ergo*, to act."*

To a sensitive nature like Pattison's, these Antinomies of the Practical Reason are at times not a curious enigma, but a painful reality. A person thus constituted can enter into Scherer's experience that *Nous cotoyons l'abîme, gare au vertige*. He has learnt that the strivings of his abnormal conscience towards its goal often need, not stimulating, but checking; and his cynical utterances, harsh and unnatural in their tone, are naught but the grating sound of the drag which is put on the wheel.

In referring to the father of all sceptics, whose treatise by means of a felicitous forgery has made its way into the Canon of Scripture, Renan oddly remarks : " La bonté du sceptique est la plus solide de toutes ; elle repose sur un sentiment profond

* See also the fifth stanza of *The Higher Courage*. In *The Latest Decalogue*, the contrast is marked between ideal and conventional morality :—

> " Thou shalt not covet, but tradition
>   Approves all forms of competition."

de la vérité suprême, *Nil expedit*."* I pointed
out this sentence to Pattison, who seemed to
regard it with something of approval. But he
would doubtless have admitted that the word
bonté must be referred rather to public than to
private virtue—must be taken to denote not
heroism, but *kindliness*. So interpreted, the
words may be applied to Pattison himself.
Charles Austin was fond of a saying of Voltaire to
the effect that, if one would fain work for mankind, one must avoid being disgusted with mankind, and must therefore forbear seeing too much
of ordinary men and women. It is perhaps safer
to assert that some who devote their time and
sympathy to public objects, and all who thirst
after a wide popularity, impair their capacity for
contracting close friendships—for making a few
men and women feel that they take a personal

* Again, in *L'Antechrist*, p. 101, he describes *Ecclesiastes*
as a " livre charmant, le seul livre aimable qui ait été composé par un Juif ;" and adds (p. 102),—" Nous ne comprenons
pas le galant homme sans un peu de scepticisme ; nous
aimons que l'homme vertueux dise de temps à autre, *Vertu,
tu n'es qu'un mot*." He goes on to say that the power of
smiling at one's own work is " la qualité essentielle d'une
personne distinguée," and maintains that this quality was
strikingly exemplified in Christ. I wish that some reader
would inform me what saying or sayings of Christ, Renan
could possibly have had in his mind when he made this
startling assertion.

F

interest in them. Pattison achieved this, though he laboured under a great drawback. Study engrossed much of his time and interest; and, perhaps on that account, he was at the close of his life lacking in power of sympathy. May it not have been because his small disposable fund of time and sympathy was seldom drawn upon for mankind in the aggregate, that he had any time or sympathy to spare for the few women and fewer men whom he really valued? At any rate, his misanthropy, or rather his *aphilanthropy*, freed him from that last infirmity of noble reformers—intolerance of human frailty. Other causes might be mentioned; but the foregoing may serve to explain how it was that the Rector enjoyed the privilege—a privilege rarely vouchsafed to such a hard student—of inspiring the few whom he admitted to his friendship with a larger measure of, not admiration merely, but affection. It may not be amiss to record a curious instance of the enthusiasm which he once excited in an unexpected quarter. One of his old pupils writes : "For part of my time, Pattison's scout was also mine. He was the only honest, manly, true-hearted man as a college scout that I ever knew, and he almost adored Pattison." One fact may serve to explain the scout's devotion to his master. Pattison strongly disapproved of the complete separation which, in English households especially, subsists between masters and servants. When sociably inclined, he made spasmodic attempts to break through the barrier.

It was with some surprise that I learnt at Biarritz how unknown Pattison was, even by name, to most of the travelling English. There was something at once instructive and humbling in the question that I heard asked, " Do you know that there is a brother of Sister Dora in the hotel ?"—implying that he was doomed to Lethe, and that no one but his sister could rescue him even for a short space (*Juturnam misero succurrere fratri*). Being consulted by an undergraduate as to what he should do in the way of study, Pattison startled his questioner by answering (in effect), " Take care of *what you are*, and *what you do* will take care of itself." The world is happily determined to apply this principle to Pattison,—to judge him, not by what he did, but by what he was, and not to let him be written down even by himself. One of his kinsfolk, who had ample means of judging, assures me that his disappointment in 1851 "weighed upon his memory " far more during his last illness than it had done for many years before. He had, in fact, lived to become a mere—

ἄθλιον

εἴδωλον, οὐ γὰρ δὴ τόδ' ἀρχαῖον δέμας.

This may partly explain the defects of his *Memoirs;*
for it is, I think, just as well as generous to refer
in great measure to his morbid condition the deplorable domestic and academic disclosures, and the
more deplorable exaggerations about Conington
which deface that unfortunate volume.*

> "If 't be so,
>   Hamlet is of the faction that is wronged,
>   His madness is poor Hamlet's enemy."

The Rector was never very misanthropical when
talking to me ; perhaps he thought misanthropy
would not be good for me. Shortly after we
parted at Biarritz, he wrote about me to a lady
friend (the inscription is *bilingual,* being on a
post-card) :—" Pray present my compliments to
our *philosophe errant,* and prevail upon him to *se*

---

* So far from becoming a bigoted Puseyite after his "con-
version," Conington was to the last very tolerant. I asked
him (in or about 1857) what he thought of a contemptuous
attack on Mr. Congreve which had recently appeared in the
Times. He replied that he liked far better an article in the
Saturday Review, which, while differing from Mr. Congreve's
views, treated him with consideration. On another occasion,
one of his Liberal friends (some of his friends were strong
Liberals) informed him in my presence that I had ventured
to tell that Tory assembly, the Oxford Union, that we owed
a debt of gratitude to Carlyle for importing into England a
taste for German theology. Conington merely looked at me
and said, with an amused smile, " Really, really." I have
elsewhere recorded his great admiration for Mill.

détendre un peu plus, if he wishes to keep the machine in good order." It may have been with a like feeling of goodwill that, knowing or fancying that I am wont to take too grave and sad a view of human life, he put (so to speak) into his conversation with me little of the spirit of Timon and much of the spirit of Montaigne; just as Horace infused into Odes addressed to the comrades of his youth a mild Epicureanism as an antidote to Republican zeal.

Thirteen years ago, I asked a distinguished Oxonian to tell me whom he thought the foremost man in the University. "Jowett," he replied, "has a touch of genius, which Pattison has not; otherwise, taking him all round, Pattison is the first man in Oxford." I would venture to add that (still perhaps excepting Mr. Jowett) he was the first clergyman of our time. Not, of course, that his tastes were those of his clerical brethren. A Scotch book called *Natural Law in the Spiritual World*, which has had a "mad success" with old maids, clergymen, and homœopathic doctors, was sent to him, perhaps in order to convert him. Not relishing its author's *naïve* attempt to keep the newest wine in cracked bottles, and also to found on the wholesale immorality of natural forces analogies such as might more consistently be used to defend the religion of Juggernaut than the religion of Jesus, he said drily to a friend, " I don't think this book will suit us," and contemptuously threw it aside.* In talking with him one day, I expressed surprise at the almost universal obscurantism of the Bishops. " It is quite natural," he said. " After a man has been consecrated ten years, he loses all sympathy with the modern spirit. No ; there is one exception. The Bishop of —— sometimes sits next me at luncheon at the Athenæum,† and asks simple questions, just like a little boy, about evolution and other modern speculations. This Bishop really tries to keep pace with the modern spirit ; but he is the only one." He, however, emphatically pronounced Dean Stanley to be a " thorough Liberal," a circumstance which seemed to surprise him on account of the Dean's imaginative and perhaps unscientific cast of mind. Pattison's summary condemnation of the Anglican Bishops was probably meant to be taken more or less in jest. But he was speaking quite seriously when

---

* A writer in the *Contemporary Review* for March passes a yet severer judgment on the book ; he stigmatizes its author's theory as " neither science nor theology, but a bastard Calvinism of which Scotland ought to be ashamed." Is *legitimate* Calvinism much better ?

† The Rector said that the library of the Athenæum " is the most delightful place in the world—especially on a Sunday morning."

he pronounced a very similar judgment on a far more formidable body of ecclesiastics. I asked him whether he did not expect that, at no distant period, some wise Pope and Cardinals will (by a now familiar device) seek to disburden Catholicism of the belief in hell—whether, in fact, they will not demonstrate that the Popes who sanctioned that unsavoury doctrine were not speaking *ex cathedrâ*, or were misreported, or that the question lies beyond the province of Papal Infallibility; or, at any rate, that *Nullum tempus occurrit Deo* (see 2 Peter iii., 8), and that every expedient which is used to show that the numerous plain texts which seem to predict the immediate end of the world do not really mean what they seem to mean, will equally show that the texts and other Catholic authorities which seem to predict the endlessness of hell need not mean what they seem to mean.* " No," replied he; " Catholicism will not change. The Cardinals have no conception whatever of the intellectual changes going on in the world. They often show ability in diplomatic matters, but in nothing else." Yet, though untainted by the ecclesiastical virus, he was to the last a clergyman in the best sense.

* Tillotson (*l.c.*), after quoting Jonah iii. 10, to prove that God may be better than his word, raises the delicious question : Would he also be better than his oath (Ps. xcv. 11) ?

He rather surprised a friend by making the broad statement that mankind will never be able to dispense with religious observances. He was thereupon reminded that "never" is a far-reaching word, and was asked whether he did not think that, at some very remote epoch, the temptations to crime may be so much lessened, and public opinion may be so much better organized, that morality will be able to stand on its own bottom. " I accept the correction," he answered frankly; " such a time *may* come; but, if it ever is to come, it is now so extremely distant that we and our children will only get into trouble by taking it into practical consideration."

My readers may remember Pattison's observation that the idea of Deity has now been "defecated to a pure transparency."* This queer metaphor will serve as an introduction to his views on the two foundation-stones of Natural Theology. I asked him whether he thought that either Mr. Stopford Brooke or Mr. Voysey is likely to have much permanent influence. He answered in the negative; in the present state of opinion, most of those whose temperament leads them to reject what Mr. Stopford Brooke and Mr. Voysey agree in rejecting, will not accept what

* Quoted by Mr. Harrison, *Nineteenth Century*, Vol. xv., p. 496.

they agree in accepting. In short, the stream of tendency is towards Agnosticism. I asked what he thought of the logical strength of Agnosticism; and, by way of drawing him out, I stated as forcibly as I could the argument which Mr. Grote —the "rigid Atheist," as he was called in Benthamite circles — would certainly have used against it. Mr. Grote would have insisted that there is not a tittle of evidence to show that fairies do not exist, and yet that, as soon as it became manifest that there is no evidence to show that they do exist, the case went against them by default; we do not merely *doubt* their existence, we *deny* it. In like manner, Mr. Grote applied to all spiritual beings the maxim that *Entia non sunt multiplicanda praeter necessitatem*, and he would have contended that, just as Unitarianism has been called a feather bed to catch a falling Christian, even so Agnosticism is a feather bed to catch a falling Theist.* When I laid this reason-

---

* An eminent jurist and philosopher, after reading this paragraph, asked me how we could possibly *deny* the existence of fairies. I answered that by the word "fairies" I mean spiritual beings able and willing to act in a specified manner on human affairs. If junkets mysteriously disappear, their owner unhesitatingly attributes the disappearance to thieves, mice, or some other natural agency; in other words, he denies that there exists any "fairy Mab" able and willing to steal junkets. In like manner, we may confidently deny that there exists a Spiritual Being who is able and willing

ing before Pattison, I found to my amazement that it was quite unfamiliar to him. In answer to it, he merely quoted with approval the words of a Greek sage (I think Protagoras) : Θεοὶ εἰ εἰσὶν ἤ εἰ μὴ εἰσὶν ἄδηλον.

An Oxford contemporary and friend of Pattison's, the late Sir Benjamin Brodie, used to quote approvingly a very similar passage from Faust :—

> " Wer darf ihn nennen ?
> Und wer bekennen :
> Ich glaub' ihn ?
> Wer empfinden
> Und sich unterwinden
> Zu sagen : Ich glaub' ihn nicht ?"

It may serve to throw light on the Rector's state of mind, and perhaps, too, on the theological tendencies of the University, if I advert for a moment to Brodie's opinions on these subjects. He called himself an A. L. (Advanced Liberal). Like Pattison, he was sceptical about miracles. In rebuking a friend whom he deemed too credulous, he exclaimed, " You'll tell me next that you believe that the serpent climbed up the tree and began talking to Eve." Yet he told me that Comte's *Positive Philosophy* seemed to " throw a wet blanket " over him ; and he rather startled

to modify Natural Laws, even with a view to the prevention of sin and sorrow.

me by expressing regret at the line taken by Professor Tyndall in the *Belfast Address.* He insisted that Berkeley's Theory has never been refuted (though I doubt whether the Bishop would have acknowledged him as a disciple). His meaning probably was that, while believing in the absolute uniformity of Natural Laws, he yet thought (as Mr. Romanes thinks) that the ultimate *causa causarum*, the basis of phenomena, may be Spiritual and Intelligent. " The real puzzle is," he used to say, " how *anything* comes to exist," — anything whatever, either Mind or Matter. He once expressed a belief or hope that the course of Nature is directed by " Infinite Wisdom "; and, on being asked how he reconciled Infinite Wisdom with the existence of evil, he replied that we do not quite know what the word " infinite " means. These opinions of the late Professor of Chemistry are more optimistic than those commonly expressed by Pattison; but they may illustrate them by pointing to a *modus vivendi*—seemingly the only one—between Theism and modern science. Though I could not persuade either Brodie or Pattison to expound their views fully, I should conjecture that they were something of this sort :—

" Nature, indeed, is profoundly immoral; with reckless impartiality, she gives her sunstrokes to the evil and to the good, and causes her floods to descend on the just and on the unjust. Yet it is this same immoral agent which, by yielding suitable conditions, has led to the evolution of all our moral sentiments, and may lead to the evolution of yet higher moral sentiments among posterity. For aught we know, those moral sentiments could not have been evolved by any less painful process."

Yet, though Pattison refused to acquiesce in Grote's dogmatic negation, he relinquished a belief which was till lately regarded as a necessary adjunct of Theism, but which some disciples of Dr. Martineau are now prepared to give up. I reminded him of the havoc which the modern belief in the absolute uniformity of Natural Law is making with the older belief, the belief in supernatural intervention; and I asked him whether he did not feel a difficulty in reconciling the modern belief with the belief in the greatest of all miracles, the Miracle of Creation.* "Yes," he answered thoughtfully, " I suppose that Pantheism is the only form of Theism which can be reconciled with Evolution." Pantheism is an ugly word, and also a very vague one. I imagine that, in using it,

---

* In my *Safe Studies*, pp. 390, 391, this argument is stated more fully, almost in the words in which it wa addressed to the Rector.

Pattison merely meant to express a view identical with Goethe's :—

> "Was wär' ein Gott, der nur von aussen stiesse,
> Im Kreis das All am Finger laufen liesse,
> Ihm ziemt's die Welt im Innern zu bewegen,
> Natur in Sich, Sich in Natur zu hegen,
> So dass, was in Ihm lebt und webt und ist,
> Nie Seine Kraft, nie Seinen Geist vermisst."

As in regard to Theism, so in regard to the belief in immortality, Pattison (like Renan) declined to deduce the negative conclusion which some might have drawn from his premisses. He spoke indeed differently at different times. Sometimes his view seemed to be a depressing one. For instance, he once startled me with the query, "Shall I have my library in heaven?"—a question in reply to which I certainly was unable to give more definite information than he himself possessed, but which somehow conveyed the notion that he regarded a posthumous library and a posthumous life as equally improbable, or at any rate that he would find the latter tedious without the former. So, again, in a touching and mournful letter which he wrote to me three weeks before he died, he said, "I am approached very near now to the 'fabulae Manes et domus exilis Plutonia.'" And we learn with pain that, as his end drew near, the shadows became yet darker.

But he would assuredly have maintained that his
real views were those which he held in the fulness
of health, though even in health a man of his
temperament may have forebodings that the ghost
of his old belief will haunt him in the last scene,

"Pale and pitiful now, but terrible then to the dying";

in other words, that posthumous fears will over-
whelm him in the sad hour when the impressions
of childhood are often relatively the strongest,
and when the nerves are so weakened and the
thoughts are so uncontrolled that even the
mightiest of spiritual reformers are tempted to
utter the cry of loneliness and despair, "My God,
my God, why hast thou forsaken me?"*   When
Pattison was at his best, his anticipations in re-

* Suppose an angel (or devil) were to offer us the choice
between painless annihilation and the necessity of drawing
from a prophetic lottery containing 1000 tickets marked
heaven and one ticket marked *hell*: most of us, I conceive,
would prefer the euthanasian alternative to the risk, the
extremely small risk, of everlasting torments.   And may
not a dying philosopher, *whose nerves have been unstrung by
illness*, be excused if he shudders at the very barest possibility
that the belief in posthumous discomfort, a belief held by
some persons as honest and as learned as he is, may be well
founded, and if he is tempted to follow the example of the
numerous penitents, from Cephalus to Littré, who at the
eleventh hour

"advertunt animos ad religionem, . . .
Aeternas quoniam pœnas in morte timendum est"?

gard to immortality were such as might be resolved into the formula, *Aut caelum aut nihil ;*
he refused to close the door on religious hope.
Goethe has well said that *Man is always more
anthropomorphic than he thinks.* It is equally
true—indeed, it is another aspect of the same
truth—that Man is always more optimistic than
he thinks. And perhaps it was in consequence of
an irrepressible aspiration that a passage of Tennyson which exactly expressed Pattison's own
relation to those whom he had loved and lost,
suggested itself, when the news of his death came,
to one at least of his sorrowing friends :—

> "It may be that the gulfs will wash us down,—
> It may be we shall touch the Happy Isles,
> And see the great Achilles whom we knew."

In conclusion, we will turn from this cheerless
subject to one or two of the Rector's criticisms
on life, which show him at his best. To a friend
who complained that old age made our pleasures
less numerous and less vivid, he answered, in a
spirit worthy of Cato Major : "What we lose in
the number and vividness of our pleasures, we
gain in διάνοια: we set a juster value on those
which remain to us."

When I saw Charles Austin for the last time,
he was less of a pessimist than I had ever known
him ; and likewise to Pattison, just before his

fatal illness began, there was vouchsafed a sort of Indian summer. He was more cheerful than usual, and yet he had a presentiment that his days were numbered. " I never," he said, " felt life to be so precious as now when it is ebbing away."* He was talking to one whom he had every reason to love and value; so he laid aside reserve and took a retrospect of his career. Enlarging on a topic which cannot but recall the choice of Solomon, he gave reasons for thinking that, if he had coveted wealth or worldly distinction, he might have secured either or both. But he had preferred the path of knowledge. " I am glad," he concluded, " that I made this choice; and, if with my present experience I could live my life over again, I would lay it out on the same lines." Adapting his Master's words, he might have said :—*Unum est necessarium. Optimam partem elegi, quae non auferetur a me.*

* He was thus confirming from personal experience a saying of Goethe's which he used often to quote : " Life resembles the Sibylline book; it becomes dearer the less there remains of it." Does not this explain the anomaly, that some permanent invalids say that they would willingly live their lives over again, while many strong persons foolishly declare that they would not ? He who knows that his life is precarious, feels that it is priceless.

NOTE.

"They also serve who only stand and wait."—MILTON.

IN reference to the observations made in this article as to the interest taken by Pattison in Amiel's *Journal Intime*, M. Scherer published in the *Times* (June 2, 1885) the following letter addressed by Pattison to himself :—

"Richmond, Yorkshire, *July* 9, 1883.

" Dear Sir,—It is so long since we met that I have felt some hesitation as to addressing you by letter, lest in the crowd of new faces and figures your memory should fail to recognize me.

"The occasion of my writing is the *Journal of Amiel*, of which you are the editor. I wish to convey to you, Sir, the thanks of one at least of the public for giving the light to this precious record of a unique experience. I say unique, but I can vouch that there is in existence at least one other soul which has lived through the same struggles, mental and moral, as Amiel. In your pathetic description of the " volonté qui voudrait vouloir, mais impuissante à se fournir à elle-même des motifs "—of the repugnance for all action— the soul petrified by the sentiment of the infinite, in all this I recognise myself !

"' Celui qui a déchiffré le secret de la vie finie, qui en a lu le mot, est sorti du monde des vivants, il est mort de fait.'

" I can feel forcibly the truth of this, as it applies to myself !

"It is not, however, with the view of thrusting my egotism upon you that I have ventured upon addressing you. As I cannot suppose that so peculiar a psychological revelation will enjoy a wide popularity, I think it a duty to the editor to assure him that there are persons in the world whose souls respond, in the depths of their inmost nature, to

G

the cry of anguish which makes itself heard in the pages of these remarkable confessions.

"Believe me to be, dear Sir, yours faithfully,

"MARK PATTISON."

I am tempted to follow M. Scherer's example by inserting a letter written by Pattison to me on receipt of my "Safe Studies." It is not without scruple that I print it even for private circulation, owing to the personal reference in the last sentence. But the whole letter seems to me instructive and characteristic of its author, and, as I have already quoted its most paradoxical and cynical expressions it is perhaps fair to show from the context that Pattison at times used language far removed from paradox and cynicism.

"Lincoln College, Oxford, *January* 13, 1884.

"My dear Sir,—The literary event of the week has been your book—a stirring event to a sick man almost confined to his sofa. I have been reading, reading for three days, and have gone through the whole (except the Engadine), much of it more than once. The level of the collected papers stands so high, that I now regret the volume was not published—for your credit that is, since, as a collector, an unpublished volume is five times as precious to me. The material aspect of the book is worthy, in binding, paper, and type, of its author. But how could you give in to the American plan of cutting down the margin; a plan which makes it impossible to have a book bound, when its cloth cover shall be used up?

"If I may venture on a general remark, I should say that the papers, as a whole, show a union which is very uncommon, of two opposite qualities, viz., a dominant interest in speculation of a wide and human character, with vast resources in the memory, of single facts, incidents, or *mots*, of famous men. How, with your eyesight, you ever compassed such a range of reading, as is here brought to bear at all points of your argument, must be matter of wonder. It seems as if you could draw at pleasure upon all literature, from the Classics down to Robert Montgomery and Swinburne. In this respect, I desiderate references in the footnotes to the sources, that one might have the great pleasure of turning out the citations in their original place. But no doubt it would have been difficult for you, where you are, destitute of books, to have supplied these in many cases. Had I been in health I could have revelled in a notice, through many columns of the *Academy;* but, in my present condition, it is not possible for me to undertake any literary work, even of the lightest kind. If I now venture upon making some small notes upon single passages, you must not suppose that I am setting up to correct you, but am only desirous to show with what attention I have read you. In page 12, I feel a slight difficulty with the sentence which begins with the words, ' As the confusion.' The two ' its ' must be relative to the noun ' confusion '; then, what is the opinion meant in the concluding words of the sentence ? In page 27, I am brought up by Grote saying that the ' Geocentric theory was once as firmly held as—' Grote surely could not mean that *firmly held* is the smallest evidence of truth ? The transmutation of metals and the powers of witches were equally firmly held ; and we believe, or accept, the Heliocentric theory on its own evidence, and because the Geocentric theory has been proved* to be false, and not be-

---

* In what sense " proved "? In scientific matters, the very few experts of each generation form their own judgment indeed, but form it in accordance with the canons of evidence which are deemed conclusive in that generation. The very numerous inexperts, if they are sensible, follow the judgment of the experts : they follow it, however, not as infallible, but as less likely to be wrong than the judgment of any one else. This is true of the nineteenth century as well as of the sixteenth.—[L. A. T.]

cause it is firmly and universally held. In page 187, will you stand to the words of the bottom line, 'for the good of all men'? Do you not much rather incline to endorse Montaigne's opinion, quoted in page 116, a refreshing passage, to which I wish I had the reference in the original? In page 194, would not Disraeli's *mot* have gained in effect by giving it to him by name? In page 172, Chevalier Ramsay is injured by the prefix 'A certain'; he was a very well-known man in his day, just before or contemporary with Hume, and his books were the popular books of his day, especially 'Les Voyages de Cyprus,' an imitation of Telemachus, which was translated into all the languages on the Continent. He had an Oxford D.C.L. conferred upon him, but probably more in consideration of his Jacobitism—he was at one time tutor in the Pretender's family—than his literary repute. All that is related of Grote is most interesting; but I cannot forgive him for stigmatizing Paley as disingenuous, one of the most honest clergymen of the period. In page 209 the phrase 'more mature thinkers' implies that Tennyson is a thinker at all. Is he so? Is he not a poet, and are not poet and thinker incompatibles? In page 165, any young Curate or Priest who pronounced the Benediction over the head of his Bishop would be committing a gross breach of clerical etiquette. In page 180, did you notice that you were speaking of the *Quarterly Review* as a contemporary, though I suppose you intended to discard in what are now 'Studies' the original form of article? In page 223, 'the saying of a great orator' (who?) of the House of Lords that it is 'not made for perpetuity,' had already appeared on page 175.

"By this time I must have tired your patience with my trivial remarks, of which I hope you will take as little notice as they deserve. I have had to explain to everyone, to whom I have shown the book, the meaning of the title 'Safe.' It is, I say, a *vox praegnans, immo gravida, e cujus sinu proles altera, prodigiosa, periculosa, damnosa, exitura sit!* As for those people whose feet were cold because they washed them, it is no doubt quite true, but then they washed them in warm water; had they bathed them every morning in cold water, they would have been as warm as the dirty man's. That is a melancholy sentence with which your preface concludes. Though it is by no means my view that a man should be always producing books, or putting his thoughts in print, yet he cannot renounce a life which has hitherto been one of moral and philosophical discussion, without falling to a lower grade in the rational scale. For my part, I cannot expect ever to see you again; and I must be content with here recording my experience that your conversation was to me more stimulating than that of any man I ever met.—With kind regards,

" Believe me to be,

" Sincerely yours,

" MARK PATTISON."

Even the far too friendly expression of opinion in the concluding sentence has a biographical value as testifying to its author's sympathetic kindliness—a quality for which, among men at least, he had little credit. In reply, I ventured to point out what seemed to me one or two oversights. For example, I explained that, when I spoke of a young Curate pronouncing the Benediction in the presence of an Archbishop, I was assuming the Archbishop not to be taking any part in the service, but merely to be one of the congregation. I touched also on private matters; and at last, with real emotion, I thanked Pattison for all his kindness and bade him farewell—

> . . . *spargens flores et functus inani Munere.*

London: Printed by C. F. Hodgson & Son, 1 Gough Square, Fleet Street.

www.ingramcontent.com/pod-product-compliance
Lightning Source LLC
Chambersburg PA
CBHW032349020726
47499CB00008B/2676